The Boxcar Children® Mysteries

THE MYSTERY GIRL

created by

GERTRUDE CHANDLER WARNER

Illustrated by Charles Tang

ALBERT WHITMAN & Company
Morton Grove, Illinois

Library of Congress Cataloging-in-Publication Data
Warner, Gertrude Chandler, 1890-
The mystery girl / created by Gertrude Chandler Warner;
illustrated by Charles Tang.
p. cm. — (The Boxcar children mysteries)
Summary: While helping run Jerry Taylor's general store,
the Alden children investigate his mysterious employee Nancy.
ISBN 0-8075-5370-0 (hardcover).
ISBN 0-8075-5371-9 (paperback).
[1. Mystery and detective stories.]
I. Tang, Charles, ill. II. Title.
PZ7.W244Mvm 1992   92-14327
[Fic]–dc20   CIP
                                     AC

Cover art by David Cunningham.

Contents

CHAPTER 1

Surprises

It was summer vacation, and the Alden children, Henry, Jessie, Violet, and Benny, had gone to stay for a week with their Aunt Jane in Elmford. On the first morning of their visit, they got up early. They had decided to surprise Aunt Jane by making a special breakfast.

"I vote for pancakes," six-year-old Benny whispered as they all went quietly downstairs.

"That sounds good to me," said Henry, who was fourteen. "Pancakes with that special maple syrup that Aunt Jane gets at Jerry Taylor's general store."

"And some fresh strawberries, too," twelve-year-old Jessie said. "I saw some in the refrigerator last night when we had a snack. Benny, you can wash the strawberries, and I'll make the pancake batter."

"I'll set the table," Henry volunteered.

"And I'll pick some flowers for it," said Violet, who was ten. "Then we can all go wake Aunt Jane."

But when the Aldens went into the kitchen, Aunt Jane was already there, sitting at the table.

"Aunt Jane, it's so early!" Benny cried. "Don't you want to go back to bed for a while?"

Aunt Jane put her glass of orange juice down and smiled. "It is early, Benny, but I'm wide awake."

"Are you sure?" Benny asked. "Maybe if you got back in bed, you'd feel sleepy again."

Jessie laughed. "We'll have to wait for another time, Benny." She kissed Aunt Jane good morning. "We were going to surprise you by having breakfast ready before you got up," she explained.

"Pancakes and maple syrup and strawberries," Benny said. "It was going to be so good."

"It can still be good, Benny," Violet said. "It just won't be a surprise, that's all."

Aunt Jane shook her head. "It sounds delicious, but I'm afraid I can't take the time for a pancake breakfast this morning."

"What do you have to do?" Henry asked. He took some juice glasses from the cabinet for his brother and sisters. "Can we help?"

"I'm sure you can," Aunt Jane said. "While Andy is away on his business trip, I'm going to make some new curtains for the den." Andy Bean was Aunt Jane's husband. "It's his favorite room in the house and I just finished painting it. But the curtains are old and faded, and they look terrible."

"You're working on a surprise of your own," Violet said, as she poured orange juice for everyone.

"That's right," Aunt Jane agreed, laughing. "I thought I'd drive out to Taylor's General Store this morning. He sells everything, including fabric. Would you all like to come with me and help me pick it out?"

"Yes!" Benny took a big gulp of his juice. "We've never been there. I would really like to see it!"

Henry rumpled Benny's hair. "I bet you'd like to see all the jars of penny candy Aunt Jane told you about."

"I sure would," Benny said. "Wouldn't you?"

"You're right, I would," Henry laughed.

"Does Mr. Taylor sell peppermint drops, Aunt Jane?" Violet asked.

"Yes, he does," Aunt Jane said. "Why?"

"Because that's Grandfather's favorite candy," Violet said. "We can take him some when we go back to Greenfield."

The Aldens' parents were dead, and they lived with their grandfather, James Alden. Before that, they had run away and lived by themselves, in an old, abandoned boxcar, which they had turned into a home. They had been afraid of their grandfather because they thought he was mean and wouldn't like

them. Once they met him, they found out
how kind he was, and now they loved him
very much.

"We should take Watch something, too,"
Benny said. The Aldens' dog, Watch, had
stayed behind in Greenfield with their grandfather. "Does Mr. Taylor's store have dog
biscuits, Aunt Jane?"

"I'm not sure, Benny," Aunt Jane said.
"But he does have dog collars."

"That's perfect," Jessie said. "We'll get
candy for Grandfather and a new collar for
Watch. And here's another reason we should
go with you, Aunt Jane." She held up an
almost-empty bottle. "There's not enough of
Jerry Taylor's maple syrup left for even one
pancake."

Benny laughed. "It's a good thing you got
up before us. Aunt Jane. Pancakes without
syrup would have been a real surprise!"

After a fast breakfast of cereal with strawberries, everyone got in the car. Jerry's general store was several miles out of town. As
they were driving, Jessie pointed out the window at a long, low building with lots of glass

and a big fountain in front of it. "What's that building?" she asked. "It wasn't here the last time we came to visit you."

"That's the Elmford Shopping Center," Aunt Jane said. "It opened just a few days ago. It has several different stores in it including a grocery store, a department store that sells just about everything except food, and two restaurants."

"It looked so modern and fancy," Jessie said.

"It is," Aunt Jane said.

"Have you gone shopping there, Aunt Jane?" Violet asked.

"Not yet," Aunt Jane said. "Some of my friends have told me it's very nice, so I'll probably try it one of these days."

Soon the Elmford Shopping Center was behind them, and after a few more miles of driving, they arrived at Taylor's General Store. It was a brown wooden building with a long porch across the front. There was an old-fashioned glider on the porch, and two wooden tubs with petunias and geraniums stood beside the front door.

"This is such a pretty place," Violet said as they all got out of the car. Violet always appreciated the way things looked.

"Do you see those cabins?" Aunt Jane asked, pointing to a group of small cabins near the store. "Jerry lives in one of them, and he rents the others to people who are on vacation."

"Look!" Benny pointed to a white sign in one of the store's front windows. " 'Help Wanted,' " he read.

"I didn't know Jerry needed help," Aunt Jane said. "I was here two weeks ago and the sign wasn't there then. Jerry always has two people working for him. I wonder what happened to them."

"We'll find out soon enough," Benny said. He ran ahead of the others and hopped up the steps. As he jumped onto the porch, a tall woman came out of the store. Benny almost bumped into her, but he stopped just in time.

"Excuse me," Benny said, smiling up at the woman.

But the woman just frowned at him and

hurried down the steps, past Aunt Jane and the others.

"That woman didn't buy a thing," Aunt Jane said, as she and the others joined Benny on the porch. "I've never known anyone to leave Jerry's store empty-handed."

"Maybe she wanted to run in and ask directions," Jessie said. "She looked like she was in a hurry."

"But how could she not buy any penny candy?" Benny asked.

Henry laughed. "Maybe she just doesn't like it, Benny."

Just then, they all heard a girl's voice cry, "Oh, no! Look out!" Then there was a clanging, rattling noise from inside the store.

CHAPTER 2

The General Store

Aunt Jane and the children ran into the store. They saw a pile of shiny pots and pans lying on the floor. A woman was standing near the long wooden counter, and a young girl with short red hair was picking up the pans. Violet said, "Let's go help."

The Aldens quickly picked up the rest of the pans and put them on the counter. "Oh, thank you," said the red-haired girl. "I don't know what happened. I was reaching for a pan and suddenly they all came tumbling off the shelf. I'm just glad you didn't get hit on the head," she said to the woman who was standing by the counter.

"No harm done to me," the woman said. "Are the pans all right?"

"Oh, yes," the girl said. "Mr. Taylor sells the best." She held up a deep saucepan with a wooden handle. "You see? Not even a scratch."

The woman took the pan and looked it over. The girl smiled at the Aldens and Aunt Jane. "Mr. Taylor is on the phone in his office right now," she said. "But I'll be with you in just a moment."

"Please don't hurry," Aunt Jane told her. "I need to take my time looking at the fabric."

Aunt Jane and Violet walked over to look at the bolts of cloth on one side of the store.

On the other side of the store there were boxes of nuts and bolts and nails, gardening and building tools, and camping equipment. "This is a great place!" Henry said to Jessie. He walked over to look at the building tools.

"Aunt Jane was right," Jessie said. "This store has everything." She went to look at the shelves of sweatshirts, jeans, thick socks, and leather belts.

Near the counter was a table with fresh fruit and vegetables. There were also two big barrels, one with peanuts in the shell, the other with walnuts. On the shelves behind the counter were jars of maple syrup and honey and jam. On the counter itself was a long row of big glass jars filled with bright-colored candy. Benny stayed close to the counter and looked at the candy. He could hear the woman and the red-haired girl talking about the pans.

"This is a nice one," the woman said.

"It sure is," said the red-haired girl enthusiastically. "You will be able to make great scrambled eggs in it."

The woman laughed a little. "My dear," she said. "This is a saucepan. I might use it to *boil* eggs, but I could never scramble them in it."

The red-haired girl blushed. Then she laughed, too. "You are right," she said. "I guess I got mixed up."

Just then, a man came out of a room at the

back of the store. He was middle-aged, with thick brown hair and bright blue eyes, and he looked worried.

Aunt Jane saw him and smiled. "Hello, Jerry," she said.

Jerry Taylor stopped looking worried and smiled, too. "Hello, Jane," he said, walking over to her and Violet. "I'm glad to see you."

"It's nice to see you, too," Aunt Jane said. "I want you to meet my nieces and nephews, who are visiting me."

By this time, Benny, Jessie, and Henry had joined them. Aunt Jane introduced them to Jerry Taylor, and they all shook hands.

"Your Aunt Jane has told me a lot about you and I'm glad to meet you," Mr. Taylor said to the children. "I'm afraid I can't talk very long right now, though. I want to stay by my phone in the office. I'm hoping to get more calls about the job."

"We saw the help wanted sign in your window," Aunt Jane said. "What happened to Sam and Dick, who used to work here?"

"Sam and his family moved away," Jerry

said. "But Dick quit and went to work at the shopping center."

"That new one we passed on the way here?" Jessie asked.

Jerry nodded. He was looking worried again. "There's nothing wrong with a shopping center, of course," he said. "But it's fancy and modern, and my store is pretty old-fashioned. I can't help worrying that the Elmford Shopping Center will hurt my business."

"I don't believe it," Benny declared. "This is the *best* store I've ever seen!"

Jerry smiled. "I hope all my regular customers agree with you, Benny."

"I'm sure they will," Jessie said reassuringly.

"Have you lost much business yet?" Henry asked.

"No, not yet," Jerry said. "Of course, everyone will try the new place out. I don't blame them. But if they stick with me, I'll have to be ready for them. And that means having enough help."

Just then, the woman who had been looking at the pans walked past them and went outside.

"Gosh," Benny said. "She didn't buy anything, either."

The red-haired girl came over to Jerry and the others. She looked disappointed. "I'm sorry, Mr. Taylor," she said. "I thought for sure that woman was going to buy the pan, even though I knocked them off the shelf. But at the last minute, she said she wanted to look in some other places."

"Probably the new shopping center," Jerry said. He shook his head and then patted the girl on the shoulder. "That's all right, Nancy," he said. "I'm sure you did your best to sell it." He turned to the others. "This is Nancy Baldwin," he said. "She started working for me a week ago, and I sure am glad to have her."

"Hi, I'm Jessie Alden," Jessie said. "This is my sister, Violet, and my brothers, Henry and Benny. And this is our Aunt Jane. She lives in Elmford and we're visiting her."

Nancy smiled and shook hands with the children and Aunt Jane. But before they

could say any more than hello, the door opened and a woman came in. She started looking at the fruit.

"Excuse me," Nancy said to the Aldens and Aunt Jane. "I'd better get back to work. Cross your fingers that I don't knock anything else down!"

After Nancy walked over to the customer, a telephone rang. "Good," Mr. Taylor said. "I hope it's someone about the job. I sure do need the help." He went back into his office.

"This is too bad," Aunt Jane said as she and the children walked over to look at the bolts of fabric. "I hope Jerry finds another person to work here soon."

"He is really worried about the new shopping center, too," Violet said. "Is there anything we can do to cheer him up?"

"Let's buy lots of curtain material and candy," Benny suggested. "That will make him happy."

"'That's a good idea, Benny," Henry said, laughing. "It's too bad we can't do it every day."

Just then, a man came into the store. He

looked around and then said loudly, "Excuse
me, but I need to buy some nails, and I'm
in a big hurry."

Nancy Baldwin, who was still busy with
the other customer, said, "I'll be with you
just as soon as I can."

The man frowned. "I can't wait long. I'm
in the middle of repairing my front steps.
Where is Jerry? Can't he help me?"

"Not right now, I'm afraid," Nancy said
nervously. She was holding a bunch of bananas that the other customer had picked out.
"He should be back in just a few minutes,
though."

The man frowned even harder. Nancy
looked even more nervous and dropped the
bananas she was holding.

"Oh, no!" her customer said. "Now
they're probably bruised."

"I'm sorry," Nancy said. "Please, pick out
another bunch."

"Another bunch?" said the man who
wanted the nails. "I'm going to be waiting
here forever."

"Poor Nancy," Violet whispered. "She's

having a hard time trying to do everything herself."

"I can help out with this," said Henry. He walked over to the man and said, "I'll be glad to show you the nails."

"Do you work here?" the man asked.

Henry shook his head. "No, but I worked in a hardware store once. And I was just looking at the hammers and bolts and nails. What kind of nails do you need?"

The two of them walked over to where the nails were, and soon, Henry had helped the man find the ones he needed. Henry took the man's money and gave him his change and a receipt from the cash register.

When the man left, Nancy was ready to weigh the new bananas the woman had picked out. "Let me see," she said, "bananas are thirty-nine cents a pound." She put a small bunch of bananas on the big brass scale and stared at it. "These weigh — "

"A pound, exactly," the customer interrupted.

"You're right!" Nancy sounded relieved. "That will be thirty-nine cents."

The woman counted out the change. Henry was still at the cash register, so he opened it and Nancy put in the thirty-nine cents. Then the woman decided to look at gardening tools, so Nancy went with her. "Thanks for helping that man with the nails," she said to Henry as she left the counter. "Tell your aunt I'll be with her just as soon as I can."

"The store is pretty busy," Henry said as he joined Aunt Jane and the others. "That's good. But if Mr. Taylor doesn't find another person to work here, I'm afraid people won't want to wait until Nancy can help them."

Jessie nodded. "Then he *will* lose business, just like he said."

"He's not going to lose *your* business is he, Aunt Jane?" Benny asked.

"Of course not, Benny," Aunt Jane said. "I've been coming to his store for years and I've always been satisfied." She held the material she and Violet had been looking at. It was blue with light brown stripes running through it. "What does everyone think of this?" she asked.

Benny and Jessie said it was just right for the den, and Henry said, "I think Andy will like it a lot."

"I do, too," Aunt Jane agreed. "And Violet gave me a good idea. I'll buy some extra material and use it to cover the throw pillows on the couch."

"That's a great idea, Violet," Jessie said. "I'll help you measure the material."

"I'll pick out a dog collar," Henry said.

"And I'll get the candy," Benny volunteered eagerly.

"Good," Jessie said. "Since Nancy and Mr. Taylor are so busy, we can save them time by doing the work ourselves."

CHAPTER 3

The Aldens Get a Job

It didn't take long for Violet and Jessie to measure and cut the material. By the time they finished, Benny had filled two small bags with peppermint drops, and Henry had chosen a blue dog collar for Watch.

The children and Aunt Jane walked over to the counter and put their things on it. Nancy and her customer came over at the same time. Nancy looked very happy when she saw the curtain material all measured and cut. "Oh, thank you," she said. "That was a big help. I'll be with you in just a minute."

Nancy wrapped up the customer's gardening gloves and tools. Then she stared at
the cash register and bit her lip.

"What's the matter, Nancy?" Jessie asked.

"It's silly," Nancy said, "but I keep for-
getting how to work this cash register. The
others stores I've worked in had more modern ones."

"The hardware store where I worked had
this kind," Henry said. "I'll be glad to show
you again."

Henry rang up the sale, took the money
from the customer, and made change. Nancy
watched him closely. While they were doing
that, Violet helped Benny weigh the candy
on the scale, and Jessie and Aunt Jane figured
out how much money the curtain material
would cost. Henry took the money for everything, and made change again.

"Thank you," Nancy said. "I'm sure I
won't forget next time."

"What other kinds of stores have you
worked in?" Henry asked Nancy as she was
putting their things in a bag.

"What do you mean?" Nancy looked confused.

Henry and Jessie looked at each other. They both remembered that Nancy had just talked about working in other stores with more modern cash registers.

Nancy noticed them looking at her and laughed nervously. She said quickly, "This is my first *full-time* job. I'm nineteen and I just finished high school a year ago."

"Oh, then the others must have been after-school jobs," Henry said.

"That's right, they were!" Nancy replied.

"What kinds of jobs?" Benny asked.

"Oh, gosh, there were so many, it's hard to remember them all." Nancy was twisting the bag holding the Aldens' things. Suddenly, she dropped it. As she bent to pick it up, Henry and Jessie looked at each other again. Nancy seemed *very* nervous. Why didn't she want to talk about the other jobs she'd had?

When Nancy put the bag on the counter, Benny said, "You must like to work if you've had so many jobs."

"Maybe Nancy worked to help out with expenses," Aunt Jane suggested.

"That's right," Nancy said, looking relieved. "My family doesn't have a lot of money, and I always took jobs to help out."

"Do you still live at home?" Jessie said.

Nancy shook her head. "No, I'm on my own now," she answered.

"We were on our own once, too," Henry said. He told Nancy about their parents and described the boxcar they had lived in. "The boxcar was fun," he said, "but I'm glad we live with Grandfather now."

"He moved the boxcar to his backyard for us," Violet said. "We still have picnics in it sometimes."

"Does your family live near Elmford, Nancy?" Jessie asked.

Nancy looked nervous again. "They live far away, in another state."

"Gosh, you must miss them," Benny said.

Nancy blushed and looked down at the counter. "I do," she said softly. Then she looked up and smiled. "But being on my own is fun, like you said, Henry."

"Where do you live?" Violet asked.

"In one of Mr. Taylor's cabins," Nancy told her. "Even though it's small, it's very comfortable."

Just then, Jerry Taylor came out of his office. He looked worried again.

"Oh dear," said Aunt Jane. "It looks like Jerry still hasn't found anyone else to work here."

"What happened, Mr. Taylor?" Nancy asked as he came over to the counter.

"Well, the woman who called wanted the job," Mr. Taylor said. "But she only wanted to work for a month or so." He sighed. "I need someone who's willing to stay on."

"I'm sure you'll find somebody soon," Aunt Jane said.

"I hope so," Jerry said. "This isn't a big store, but it still takes a lot of work. Nancy can't do it all by herself, and I don't always have time to help out."

"Do you have more people coming about the job?" Jessie asked.

"Yes, I do, thank goodness," Jerry said. "I put an ad in the newspaper and people will

be coming to see me all week." He smiled at
Jessie. "Why did you ask?"

"I'll bet I know why!" Violet said excitedly. "Jessie thinks *we* could work here
until you find someone. Isn't that right,
Jessie?"

"That's exactly what I was thinking," Jessie said. "You must be a mind reader,
Violet."

Mr. Taylor looked too surprised to say
anything. But Nancy was excited. "It's a
wonderful idea, Mr. Taylor," she said.
"They've already helped out. Henry took
care of a customer when I was too busy, and
Jessie cut the material, and — "

"And Violet showed me how to use the
scale," Benny interrupted. "Now I can do it
myself."

"We can do other things for you, too,"
Henry said to Mr. Taylor. "Sweep out the
store, and put prices on things."

"I could make signs if you need them,"
Violet said, smiling shyly at Mr. Taylor. "I
like to do that."

"And she's good at it, too," Jessie said.

"Violet's the best," Benny added admiringly.

Mr. Taylor scratched his head. "It's nice of you to offer. I'm very grateful. But I just don't know," he said doubtfully. He looked at Aunt Jane. "What do you think about this?"

Aunt Jane smiled. "I think you couldn't find four better helpers anywhere," she said.

"Well . . ." Mr. Taylor scratched his head again. "It sure would take a big worry off my mind," he said. "Of course, you can't go back and forth to Elmford every day. That would take too much time."

"We could stay in one of your cabins, just like Nancy does," Jessie said.

Mr. Taylor laughed. "That's just what I was going to suggest, Jessie. You can stay in the cabin next to mine, that way I can keep an eye on you. Your aunt can come by from time to time to make sure everything's all right."

"Then you'll let us work here?" Benny asked.

Mr. Taylor laughed again. "You're hired,

Benny," he said. "All four of you."

"You won't regret it," Aunt Jane said. She picked up the bag of curtain fabric and turned to the Aldens. "We'd better drive back to Elmford now so you can pack some things."

"And call Grandfather," Violet said.

"Right," Henry agreed. "Wait until he hears we're going to be working at a general store and living in a cabin!"

"Your grandfather won't mind, will he?" Mr. Taylor asked anxiously.

"Oh, no," Jessie told him. "He's used to us doing things like this."

"Like what?" Nancy asked.

"Having adventures," Benny said as they walked toward the front door. "You'll see, Nancy. The four of us are always having great adventures!"

CHAPTER 4

The Aldens Go to Work

When the Aldens got back to Aunt Jane's house, they called Grandfather and told him about working in Mr. Taylor's store and staying in one of his cabins. Grandfather thought it was a fine idea.

"Jane told me all about Mr. Taylor," he said to Jessie on the phone. "She says he's a good friend."

"I'm glad we can help him," Jessie said.

Grandfather chuckled. "I might have known the four of you would find something special to do while you're away."

"It will be fun," Jessie said. She laughed. "Benny really likes Mr. Taylor's store, especially the candy."

Grandfather chuckled again. "Tell him not to eat too much of it," he said. "And have a wonderful time."

When everyone had spoken to Grandfather, they quickly packed some clothes to take back with them. Mr. Taylor had told them that the cabins were stocked with bedding and towels and cooking things, so they didn't need to take any of that. But Benny made sure to pack his favorite cup, the cracked pink one that he had found when they lived in the boxcar.

"This is going to be almost like living in the boxcar again," Violet said as Aunt Jane drove them back to the general store.

"Yes, except this time we won't be hiding," Jessie said. "Remember how scared we were that someone would find us and tell Grandfather about us?"

"We thought he was so mean," Henry laughed. "Were we ever wrong!"

When they reached the general store, Jerry

Taylor came out with the key to their cabin. "I'm on one side of you, and Nancy's cabin is on the other," he said, pointing. "All the other cabins are empty right now, except for the one at the far end of the row."

"Who's staying there?" Henry asked.

"A Mrs. Edwards," Mr. Taylor said. He looked around. "Her car's not here now, I guess she's out. In fact, I don't see her very often. She comes in the store once in a while, but she never buys a thing."

"Maybe she's the woman we saw this morning," Henry said. "Benny thought it was strange that she didn't come out of your store with a bag full of candy."

"It *was* strange," Benny said. "Your candy's great, Mr. Taylor. How could anybody resist it?"

Jerry Taylor laughed. "Maybe you can ask Mrs. Edwards if you see her, Benny." He handed the cabin key to Jessie. "I'm afraid I can't take the time to show you the cabin right now," he said. "Nancy's all alone in there with four customers. But if you need anything, be sure to let me know later."

"Don't worry," Jessie said. "I'm sure everything will be fine."

"We'll put our things away and be ready to work real soon," Henry said. He gestured to the others. "Come on, let's go see our cabin!"

Carrying their duffel bags, the Aldens and Aunt Jane walked down the path and stopped in front of the second cabin. It was made of weathered boards, like the general store, and it had a small porch with two old rocking chairs on it.

Violet stooped down beside the wooden front step and pointed to a small patch of flowers growing there. "Look. Wild violets."

"Your favorite flower," Jessie said with a smile. "Just like the ones on the wallpaper in your room at Grandfather's. You're going to feel right at home here."

"I think we're all going to feel at home," Henry said. He had already opened the door and looked inside. "Come and see."

The front part of the cabin was a big room with a huge stone fireplace on one wall. Near the fireplace were a couch, two chairs and a table. The stove and refrigerator and sink were on the other side of the room, and a round pine table and chairs were nearby.

There were two doors at the back. One led to the bathroom. The other opened into a small room with bunk beds in it.

"Wow!" Benny shouted, climbing up the ladder to the top bunk. "I want to sleep up here! Is that okay with everybody?"

"It's fine with me," Jessie called from the front room. "Violet just discovered that the couch opens up into a bed. We'll sleep here."

"It's fine with me, too," Henry said, joining Benny in the bedroom. "Just don't dangle your feet in my face in the morning."

Benny laughed and hung his legs over the side of the bed. Henry backed up and Benny slid onto his shoulders. Stooping low through the door, Henry carried Benny back into the front room and set him down. Then everyone quickly put their food and clothes away.

"I wonder why Nancy said her cabin was small," Henry said as they went out the front door. "Hers doesn't look any smaller than

ours. And ours is plenty big for the four of us."

Benny kicked a small rock along the path and chased after it. "Come on!" he called back over his shoulder. "Mr. Taylor said Nancy was really busy. Let's hurry and help her!"

The Aldens said good-bye to Aunt Jane, who told them she'd drive out to see them in a day or two. Then they went into the store.

"We're ready to work," Henry said to Mr. Taylor. "Tell us what to do."

"There's only one customer right now, and Nancy is helping her," Mr. Taylor said. He looked around the store. "The gardening tools need straightening out," he said. "One of the other customers didn't put anything back."

"Violet and I will do that," Jessie said.

"Good," Mr. Taylor said. "Henry and Benny, why don't you come back to the storeroom with me? A new shipment of sweatshirts and jeans just arrived. You can help me unpack them."

Mr. Taylor, Henry, and Benny went into the storeroom. Jessie and Violet straightened out the gardening tools. When they finished, they looked around for something else to do and saw Nancy Baldwin holding a big, heavy bolt of cloth.

"Am I glad to see you!" Nancy cried. "You see that woman by the counter?" she asked, lowering her voice. "She's waiting for me to cut five yards of this for her and I'm having trouble unrolling it. Jessie, you and Violet did it so easily this morning. Maybe you could help me."

"We'll be glad to," Jessie said. She and Violet took the bolt of cloth and hung it back up on its hooks. Then they unrolled it and measured it out on the yardstick that was nailed to the shelf below.

"Oh, that's how you do it!" Nancy said in surprise. "I didn't notice that yardstick before." She laughed as she cut the cloth with a pair of scissors. "I've never worked in a fabric store. I guess that's why I got confused."

"You'll be able to do it from now on,"

Jessie said. She folded the material and handed it to Nancy.

But Nancy didn't go over to the counter right away. She stayed where she was, nervously rubbing her hands on the folded material.

"What's wrong, Nancy?" Jessie asked.

Nancy blushed. "This is embarrassing, she said. "But I still have trouble working that cash register."

"I watched Henry do it this morning," Jessie said. "I think I remember how."

Jessie *did* remember. A few minutes later, the customer happily left the store.

Nancy thanked Jessie and Violet. "I guess I must seem stupid to you," she said. "I like Mr. Taylor so much, and I want to do well. But when the store is busy, I get nervous and forget things."

"You don't seem stupid at all," Violet said. "It's easy to make mistakes when you're nervous."

"And don't keep thanking us for helping you," Jessie added. "That's what we're here for." But she remembered what Nancy had

said about working in so many stores. Surely
some of those stores had gotten busy, too.
Jessie couldn't help wondering why Nancy
got so nervous and was having so much trouble in Mr. Taylor's store.

It was a busy afternoon. Mr. Taylor interviewed two more people, but neither one
of them took the job. He decided to have a
sale on gardening tools and seeds. Violet
made a sign for it. On a big piece of white
cardboard she drew a picture of a man and
woman working in a flower garden. Under-
neath, she printed the words, *Sale — Garden
Tools and Seeds* in big green letters.

"That is the best sign I've ever had," Mr.
Taylor said admiringly. "It's too good to keep
in here. I'm going to nail it outside on the
porch. That way, people driving by will see
it."

When Mr. Taylor came back in after hanging up the sign, he showed Jessie and Henry
how to put price tags on the new sweatshirts
and jeans.

As Jessie and Henry were putting the

clothes on the shelves, Mr. Taylor looked through the socks. "Hmm," he said, frowning. He looked around and saw Nancy. She was getting ready to put some potatoes on the scale for a customer. "Nancy," he said, "did you sell some socks earlier?"

"Socks?" Nancy asked nervously. "I . . . I don't think so."

"Well, anyway, I'd better order some more," Mr. Taylor said. "I thought I had ten pairs left. But I only have seven." He chuckled. "You must have sold them and just forgotten about it, Nancy."

When he said that, Nancy dropped the handful of potatoes. Jessie and Henry glanced at each other. They couldn't understand why Nancy would get so upset about three pairs of socks.

The potatoes were rolling all over the floor. "I'll get them!" Benny shouted. Laughing, he chased down every potato. He had such a good time that everyone in the store laughed with him.

Nancy laughed, too, but she looked embarrassed. "I'm such a butterfingers sometimes," she said. She told the customer to choose some new potatoes. Then she asked Benny if he could weigh them himself.

"I'm pretty sure I can," Benny said. He piled the potatoes on the scale and looked at the arrow. "Four pounds," he said. "Isn't that right?"

"Exactly right," said the customer.

"And potatoes are twenty cents a pound," Nancy said.

Benny started to count on his fingers. Then he stopped. "I can't multiply yet," he said.

"That's all right, young man," said the customer, smiling. "It comes to eighty cents." She handed Benny the money and left the store.

Henry came over and patted Benny on the shoulder. "Good work," he said. "Can you use the cash register, too?"

"Not yet," Benny said. "Would you show me how, Nancy?"

Nancy laughed nervously. "Why don't you let Henry show you?" she said. "He's better at it than I am. In fact, maybe Henry should ring up all sales while he's working here."

"That's fine with me," Henry said. He opened the cash register.

Across the room, Violet and Jessie watched Benny put the money into the register drawer. "Benny is having a good time working here," Violet said to Jessie.

Jessie didn't answer. She was looking at Nancy.

"Jessie, what are you thinking?" Violet asked.

"I think we should invite Nancy to have dinner with us tonight," Jessie said. "I like her a lot, don't you?"

"Yes. She's so friendly and she laughs a lot," Violet said. "But you were thinking something else, too, weren't you?"

"Yes, I was," Jessie said. She lowered her voice, "Violet, maybe I'm imagining it. But it seems like Nancy doesn't know *anything* about working in a store."

"But she told us she had a lot of after-school jobs," Violet said quietly.

"I know," Jessie said. "But haven't you

noticed how much trouble she has? She can't work the cash register. She didn't know how to measure cloth until we showed her the yardstick. And ever since we've been here, she's let Henry make all the change."

"I know," Violet agreed. "But she said this was a different kind of cash register than she's used to. And she told us she never worked in a fabric store. Maybe that's why she didn't know about the yardstick."

"Maybe," Jessie said doubtfully. "But Mr. Taylor told us she has been working here a week. It seems like she would have learned to do things by now."

"Maybe you're right," Violet admitted. "What do you suppose it means?"

"I don't know," Jessie said. "But I can't help thinking that something strange is going on."

CHAPTER 5

Mysteries

After the store closed for the day, the Aldens hurried back to their cabin. Nancy had agreed to come for dinner, and they wanted to get a headstart on it before she arrived.

"I'm starving," Benny said as they walked along the path. "Let's have spaghetti. And salad. And bread. And — "

"Isn't that enough?" Henry interrupted, laughing.

"No, we have to have dessert, too," Benny said.

"I bought some of Mr. Taylor's oatmeal cookies," Violet said. "Do you think Nancy will like those, Benny?"

Just as Benny was about to answer, the Aldens heard footsteps behind them. When they looked, they saw Mrs. Edwards, the woman who was staying in the last cabin. She walked up to them and stopped.

"Hello," she said. "When I went by the store earlier, I saw that the four of you are working there."

"Yes, we are," Henry said. "For a few days, anyway."

"Then you must have met the girl who's employed there, too," Mrs. Edwards said. "Isn't her name Nancy?"

The Aldens nodded.

"She's so young to be on her own," Mrs. Edwards said. "She must have family nearby."

"No," Benny said. "She told us her family lives far away."

"Oh, really?" Mrs. Edwards smiled at Benny. "What else did she tell you about herself?"

Benny started to answer, but Jessie nudged him in the arm. Why was Mrs. Edwards so interested in Nancy? "She didn't tell us very much," Jessie said. "Excuse us, but we have to go in now."

As the Aldens went into their cabin, Jessie looked back. Mrs. Edwards was watching them. She wasn't smiling anymore. Jessie noticed something else. She was carrying a big white shopping bag with green lettering that spelled *The Elmford Shopping Center*.

"Did you see Mrs. Edwards's shopping bag?" Jessie said when the Aldens had gone into their cabin. "It was from the Elmford Shopping Center."

"I wonder why she doesn't buy her things at Mr. Taylor's store," Henry said. "It's much closer."

"And I wonder why she was asking us about Nancy," Jessie said. "It was strange."

"I guess it's another mystery," Violet said. "Jessie has discovered a mystery," she told Henry and Benny.

"What?" Benny asked eagerly. "Is it a scary one?"

Jessie smiled. "No," she answered. "And it might not even be a mystery. Let's start dinner and I'll tell you about it."

Henry put a big pot of water on the stove to boil for the spaghetti. Violet made a salad, and Benny set the table. While Jessie cooked some ground beef and tomato sauce, she told them her thoughts about Nancy Baldwin.

"Nancy told us she has had a lot of jobs," Jessie said, stirring the spaghetti sauce. "But I was telling Violet that she has so much trouble doing things, like working the cash register and measuring material. She even got Benny to weigh the potatoes. Maybe she can't work the scale, either."

"I remember something else," Benny said. "This morning, she thought you could scramble eggs in a saucepan."

Violet put the salad bowl on the table. "But if she hasn't worked in many stores, I wonder why Mr. Taylor hasn't noticed," she said.

"He's probably too busy," Henry said. "And Nancy is so nice, none of the customers would complain to him about her."

"That's right, she *is* nice, Benny agreed. "I like her a lot."

"We all like her," Violet said.

"Yes," Jessie agreed. "But I can't help wondering about her. I noticed something else, too. She got so nervous when we asked about her jobs and her family."

Henry said, "She acted like she was afraid to talk about them. Or embarrassed or something."

Violet opened a package of spaghetti. "What do you think we should do, Jessie?"

"Nothing, right now," Jessie said. "We might be completely wrong about this. I think we should just wait and see."

Benny agreed. "But there's one thing we should do the minute Nancy gets here."

"What's that?" Henry asked.

"Eat!" Benny said. "I'm . . ."

"Hungry!" the others all finished for him.

When Nancy arrived, Henry put the spaghetti into the boiling water, and Violet buttered a loaf of crusty bread. The evening was warm, and Nancy was wearing shorts and a T-shirt, just like the Aldens. But on her right

hand, she also wore a ring with a dark green stone in it.

"That's a beautiful ring, Nancy," Violet said as they all sat down at the table.

Nancy looked at her ring and her face got pink. "Thank you, Violet," she said.

"It's an emerald, isn't it?" Jessie asked.

Nancy shook her head. Then she twisted the ring around so the stone didn't show. "No, it's just a cheap trinket," she said with an embarrassed smile.

Jessie and Violet looked at each other. They knew they were thinking the same thing. The ring didn't look like a cheap trinket at all.

"This is a great dinner," Nancy said enthusiastically, after they began to eat. She helped herself to a piece of bread. "I haven't eaten such good food in a long time."

"We like to cook," Jessie told her. "When we lived in the boxcar, we cooked all our own food."

"At Grandfather's, Mrs. McGregor does most of the cooking," Violet said. "But we still like to help."

"I like eating better than cooking," Benny said.

"So do I, Benny," Nancy laughed. "Who is Mrs. McGregor?" she asked.

"Grandfather's housekeeper," Henry answered.

"Really?" Nancy shook her head. "My family's housekeep . . ." She stopped and blushed again. Then she cleared her throat. "I mean," she continued, "My family's housekeeper is my mother. She does all the cooking."

"Did she teach you how to cook?" Benny asked.

"Oh, she was always too busy," Nancy said. Then she quickly changed the subject. "Tell me more about your boxcar days," she said. "It sounds so interesting."

So the Aldens told Nancy about the boxcar — how they found it and made it into a home. Nancy was fascinated and asked a lot of questions. "It sounds like you had a lot of fun," she said. "But I guess it was kind of scary sometimes, wasn't it?"

"Sometimes it was," Jessie said. "But we

had each other, and that made everything all right."

"I know you're older, Nancy," Violet said. "But I still think you're very brave to be by yourself, so far away from your family."

"Far away?" Nancy looked confused.

Violet nodded. "You said they lived in another state."

"That's right, I did!" Nancy said. "I mean, they do." She quickly reached for another piece of bread. "This is great bread," she said. "Where did you get it?"

"At Mr. Taylor's store," Jessie said. She looked at Violet. It was clear to both of them that Nancy wanted to change the subject.

"Oh, no wonder it's so good," Nancy said. For the rest of the dinner, she talked about the general store, and she didn't tell them anything more about herself.

By the time dinner was over, Benny was yawning. "Working in the store made me tired," he said.

"It makes me tired, too," Nancy said. She got up and walked to the door. "Thank you for inviting me," she told the Aldens. "I had such a good time. It's so nice to be with friends, especially at dinner."

"Eat with us tomorrow, too," Jessie said warmly. "Maybe we'll pack a picnic and eat outside."

"That will be great!" Nancy opened the door and stepped into the warm night air. "Good night!" she called back over her shoulder.

The Aldens said good night, and Henry shut the door. When he turned around, he said, "I think you're right, Jessie. I think something strange is going on. Nancy doesn't want to answer any questions about herself. And she got confused when Violet talked about her family."

"Right," Jessie agreed. "This morning she told us they lived far away. But tonight, she sounded like she had forgotten what she said about them."

"I noticed that, too," Violet said. "But maybe she has family in different places."

"Maybe," Jessie said. "But why would she get so nervous when we asked her? It's almost like she's trying to hide things about herself."

"You're right," Henry agreed, frowning. "One thing's for sure. Nancy Baldwin is a real mystery."

The next morning, the Aldens got up early. Mr. Taylor's store opened at eight o'clock and they didn't want to be late.

"No time for pancakes again," Benny said. He sounded disappointed. "Do you think we will ever have a day off, so we can make a big breakfast?"

Henry sliced a banana into Benny's bowl of cereal. "We've only worked half a day," he said. "It's too soon to take time off."

"But don't worry," Violet said to Benny. "We can have pancakes at night."

"Breakfast for dinner?" Benny said. "That sounds good." He ate a big spoonful of cereal.

Violet started to eat. Then she put her spoon down. "I couldn't stop wondering about Nancy last night," she said.

"I don't think her ring is a 'trinket,' " Jessie said. "I'm almost sure it was a real emerald."

"I am, too," Violet said. "But I think

Nancy must have a good reason for telling these stories."

"Maybe," Jessie agreed. "Should we tell Aunt Jane?"

The others thought about this. Then Henry said, "Let's wait. Nancy likes us. She knows we're her friends. Maybe she will trust us enough to tell us what's going on."

"That's what I think, too," Jessie said. She washed the cereal bowls and Henry dried them.

"Me too," Benny agreed.

"Good." Violet looked relieved. "We might scare her by telling other people about her."

"I just thought of something," Jessie said. "Remember when Benny told Nancy that the four of us are always having adventures?"

"I remember," Benny said.

"Well," Jessie said. "Wouldn't Nancy be surprised if she knew *she* was our mystery?"

It was another busy day at the general store. Mr. Taylor was glad to see so many customers. But he still hadn't found anyone to work for him.

"It's the new shopping center," he said to Jessie and Henry, who were hanging up some new leather belts. "Two of the people I interviewed decided to go to work there."

"I bet they'll be sorry," Henry said. "This is a great place to work."

"I wish I could hire you full time," Mr. Taylor said with a laugh. "Well, I'll find someone. And I should stop feeling sorry for myself. I have you Aldens to help. And I have Nancy." He patted them both on the shoulder and went into his office.

Jessie and Henry smiled at each other. On the way to the store that morning, all the Aldens had decided to help Nancy whenever they could. That way, Mr. Taylor wouldn't suspect that she wasn't sure what she was doing.

"I think it's working," Jessie said to Henry. "I weighed everything that people have bought so far. And now I think Nancy knows how to use the scale."

"I'm pretty sure she can run the cash register now, too," Henry said. "I made sure she was watching whenever I did it." He pointed to the counter. "Look, she's about to do it now."

Sure enough, Nancy was standing behind the cash register. She looked around nervously and bit her lip. Then she took a deep breath and hit a button. The drawer popped open, and Nancy put some money inside.

"I was right!" Henry whispered excitedly. "She *does* know how to do it!"

Henry smiled at Jessie, but she didn't smile back. She looked confused. "Yes, Nancy just worked the cash register," she said. "But Henry, there isn't any customer. Whose money was she putting inside?"

Henry looked around the store. Jessie was right. There weren't any customers at the moment. "I don't know," he said. "Maybe Nancy just found the money."

"Then how does she know it belongs in the cash register?" Jessie asked. "Someone might have dropped it."

"If they did, then they'll probably come

back for it," Henry said. "Maybe Nancy wants to keep it safe."

"I guess that could be it," Jessie said. But for the rest of the day, no one came back for the money.

CHAPTER 6

The Picnic

Everyone worked hard for the rest of the day. When it was time to go, they were all hungry, especially Benny.

"Nancy," Jessie said, "Mr. Taylor told us that there's a stream near here. We're going to make some sandwiches and eat by the water. Would you like to come with us?"

"I'd love to," Nancy said. "I'll bring a bag of potato chips."

"Great, I love potato chips," Benny said. "Come on, everybody!" He ran down the path. Violet ran with him.

"I'll wash up and meet you in a few minutes," Nancy said to Henry and Jessie. She hurried down the path toward her cabin.

Jessie and Henry walked more slowly. They decided not to say anything about the money. At least, not yet. "I still think a customer must have put it on the counter and then left the store," Henry said. "Then Nancy found it and put it in the cash register."

"I suppose," Jessie said thoughtfully. "But the way Nancy looked around before she put it in was strange. Like she didn't want anyone to see her."

Henry watched as Nancy let herself into her cabin. "Oh, well, let's not think about it for a while. Let's get the picnic ready and have some fun."

The picnic *was* fun. They had asked Mr. Taylor to come, too, but he had to go into Elmford that evening. That was when he told them about the stream. He said it was perfect for picnics, and he was right.

"This is such a beautiful place!" Violet exclaimed when they arrived. "Look at all the wild flowers growing here."

The stream was clear and sparkling. Flowers and willow trees grew along the banks, and there was a flat, grassy spot where they could spread their picnic blanket.

"It's not deep!" Benny pulled his shoes and socks off and stepped into the water. "But it's freezing!" he shouted, laughing.

In a minute, the others had taken their shoes off and joined Benny in the stream. For a little while they jumped back and forth across the narrow stream, splashing each other with the cold, clear water.

"Look what I found!" Henry suddenly called out. He held up an old, cracked rubber ball that had been hidden by the tall grass. "Catch, Jessie!" he cried, and tossed the ball across the stream to his sister.

Jessie caught the ball and threw it to Nancy. Nancy tossed it to Benny who threw it to Violet. The game of catch went on until Benny finally said, "Let's eat!"

"Yes, let's," Nancy agreed breathlessly. "I'm famished."

"I hope you like peanut butter sandwiches," Benny said as he helped Violet spread a blanket on the grass.

"They're one of my favorites," Nancy said. She smiled at the Aldens. "You all have such a good time together. It's fun to be with you."

Violet thought Nancy must be missing her own family, and she felt sad for her. "Well, we argue sometimes."

Benny realized that Violet was trying to make Nancy feel better. "That's right, we do argue," he said. "Henry and I had an argument last week."

"That's because you wanted to play checkers and I wanted to finish reading a book," Henry said.

"Who won?" Nancy asked. She was smiling now.

"He did!" Henry and Benny said together.

"You both did," Jessie said. "Henry finished the book, and then they played checkers."

Everyone laughed, and then they set the food out on the blanket. There were sandwiches, Nancy's potato chips, grapes and ap-

ples, and some more of Mr. Taylor's oatmeal cookies.

"We're missing something," Benny said, looking at the picnic dinner. "There's nothing to drink."

"There's water from the stream," Jessie suggested. "But even though it looks clean, it might not be clean enough."

Benny put his socks and shoes on. "I'll go back to the cabin and fill a thermos with milk," he said. "Peanut butter sandwiches taste best with milk, anyway." He ran off.

"I wonder if he'll remember to bring some paper cups," Violet said. "I'll go after him, just in case."

Violet quickly caught up with Benny, and the two of them walked together. When they reached the path that led to the cabins, Benny stopped so suddenly that Violet bumped into him.

"What's the matter?" she asked.

"Look," Benny said quietly. He pointed toward Nancy's cabin.

Violet gasped a little and put her hand on Benny's shoulder. Standing in front of Nan-

cy's cabin was Mrs. Edwards. She was staring at the cabin. Then she looked up and
down the path, but she didn't see the two
Aldens.

As Benny and Violet watched, Mrs. Edwards went up the step onto Nancy's porch.
She looked back and forth again. Then she
walked over to the front window, cupped her
hands against the glass, and peered inside.

"What should we do, Violet?" Benny
asked.

"Nothing right now, Benny," Violet whispered. "Just wait."

In a moment, Mrs. Edwards stepped back
from the window. Then she left Nancy's
cabin, walked down the path, and went into
her own cabin.

Benny let out a big breath. "That was a
little scary, Violet."

Violet kept her hand on Benny's shoulder
as they walked to their cabin. "Mrs. Edwards
didn't really do anything bad."

"We should tell Nancy, shouldn't we?"
Benny asked.

"Let's tell Henry and Jessie first," Violet

said. "I want to know what they think."

Benny agreed, and the two of them got the milk and cups and went back to the others. But for Violet and Benny, the picnic wasn't as much fun as before.

Later that night, Henry and Jessie built a fire in the big stone fireplace. When they all sat down in front of it, Jessie and Henry told Benny and Violet about seeing Nancy put the money in the cash register.

"It was so strange," Jessie said.

"We saw something strange, too," Violet said.

"Strange and sort of scary," Benny added.

"What was it?" Henry asked.

Violet told them about seeing Mrs. Edwards, and how she'd looked in Nancy's cabin window.

"Why was it scary, Benny?" Henry asked.

Benny frowned. "Because of the way she acted," he said.

"I know what Benny means," Violet said. "Before Mrs. Edwards went up on the porch, she looked all around. And she did the same thing before she looked in Nancy's window. I think she didn't want anyone to see her."

"Like she was sneaking," Benny said. "Like she was doing something wrong."

"That's exactly what it was like," Violet agreed.

"And that's the way Nancy acted with the money," Jessie said.

"Maybe Mrs. Edwards and Nancy know each other. Maybe Mrs. Edwards was just looking to see if Nancy was in her cabin," Henry said.

"Nancy has never said anything about her," Jessie said. "And Mrs. Edwards doesn't seem to know Nancy. Remember, she asked us about her."

Benny was sitting cross-legged on the floor, his chin in his hands. "But we never asked if they knew each other," he said.

Jessie had to laugh. "You're right, Benny. We haven't."

"Maybe we should," Henry said. He stared thoughtfully into the fire. "Maybe we should ask Nancy about *everything*."

The others thought about it. Then Jessie

said, "But what if Nancy *is* trying to hide something? What do you think she would do if we started asking lots of questions?"

"I know what I would do," Benny said, yawning. "I would run away."

"We don't want Nancy to do that," Violet said quickly. "Maybe she's in some kind of trouble. If she is, we should help her."

Benny yawned again. "Can we help her tomorrow? I'm too sleepy to do anything tonight."

"Good idea, Benny," Henry said with a smile. He took Benny's hand and pulled him to his feet. "Come on, let's all go to sleep. Maybe we will wake up with some ideas."

Benny went to sleep right away. But after he helped make sure the fire was out, Henry lay awake in his bottom bunk for a long time. In the big front room on the open couch, Jessie and Violet lay awake, too. The three of them were all trying to think of what they should do about Nancy Baldwin.

CHAPTER 7

Worries About Nancy

At seven o'clock in the morning, Jessie and Violet were awakened by a knock on the door. Jessie threw back the soft yellow quilt and got out of bed. She peered out the window and then hurried to open the door.

"Aunt Jane!" she said, giving her aunt a hug. "Violet, Benny, Henry!" she called out, "Aunt Jane's here!"

Violet was already out of bed, and in a few minutes, Henry and Benny came in from the back room. Everyone was happy to see Aunt Jane.

"I didn't mean to wake you," Aunt Jane said, sitting down at the table. "But I got up very early this morning missing you. So I decided to drive out and see how you are."

"We're great," Benny said. "Working in Mr. Taylor's store is fun. I know how to use the scale now."

"Good for you, Benny," Aunt Jane said. She smiled at everyone. "Jerry was in Elmford last evening and he stopped by for a few minutes. He said the four of you are doing fine work."

Jessie poured some orange juice for everyone. "Have you made the curtains for the den yet?" she asked.

"I'm almost finished," Aunt Jane said. "They're going to look wonderful."

"I can't wait to see them," Violet said. "Andy is going to be so surprised."

"Yes, he is," Aunt Jane agreed, looking pleased. "Oh, I spoke to your Grandfather on the phone last night. He sends all of you his love."

"I miss him," Benny said. "Does he miss us?"

"Of course he does, Benny," Aunt Jane said.

"He's going to want us to come back to Greenfield soon," Henry said. "I hope Mr. Taylor finds someone to work in the store before we have to leave."

"I hope so, too," Aunt Jane said. "I've been talking to people in Elmford about the job. Maybe someone will be interested in it."

Jessie looked at the clock on the stove. "We better hurry and have breakfast," she said. "It's almost time to go to work."

"Can we have pancakes tonight?" Benny asked. "We *still* haven't had pancakes," he told Aunt Jane. "Violet said we could have them for dinner."

"That sounds good," Aunt Jane said. "And that reminds me. When we came out here the other day, I forgot to buy some more maple syrup. So I'll go along to the store with you when you're ready."

The Aldens ate a breakfast of fruit, toast with honey, and milk. Then they got dressed and walked to the general store with Aunt Jane.

Jerry Taylor was sweeping the porch when the Aldens and Aunt Jane arrived. "Good morning," he said with a smile.

"I came to buy some of your delicious maple syrup, Jerry," Aunt Jane said. "It looks like I'm your first customer of the day."

"The first of many, I hope," Mr. Taylor said. He suddenly looked worried.

"You aren't losing business, are you?" Aunt Jane asked.

"There were a lot of customers yesterday," Jessie said.

"You're right, Jessie. But not all of them buy things," Mr. Taylor said. "And everyone keeps talking about the new shopping center."

"I went there yesterday to see what it was like," Aunt Jane said. "It certainly is fancy. But it is also very expensive. And the things they sell aren't any better than what I can find right here."

Mr. Taylor smiled again. "You're not only my first customer, Jane," he said. "You're my best customer."

Everyone went into the store then. Aunt

Jane bought the syrup and stayed for a while, talking to the Aldens. Then she looked at her watch. "I think I'd better get back," she said. "It's almost an hour's drive to Elmford, and I want to finish those curtains today."

"Come back and see us again soon," Jessie said.

"I will," Aunt Jane promised. She gave all the Aldens a hug, and said good-bye.

Soon after Aunt Jane left, a farmer drove up in his truck. Henry helped him unload the fresh tomatoes he had brought. Jessie and Violet put them on the table in the store. Benny dusted the counter and made sure all the candy jars were full.

"A man's coming soon about the job," Mr. Taylor said to the Aldens. "Nancy told me that he called yesterday." He stopped talking and looked around. "Where *is* Nancy?"

Henry looked around too. "I've been so busy, I didn't even notice that she wasn't here."

"I hope she isn't sick," Jessie said. "I'll go to her cabin and see."

"I'll go with you," Violet said.

"If she isn't feeling well, tell her to stay in bed," Mr. Taylor called after the two girls.

But Nancy wasn't sick. When Jessie and Violet knocked on the door, Nancy opened it and smiled. But her short red hair was not combed, she had only one shoe on, and she was holding her toothbrush.

"I overslept!" she cried, pulling the door open wider. "My clock stopped during the night and the alarm didn't go off. It's a brand-new clock, too!"

"We were afraid you were sick," Jessie said as she and Violet stepped inside.

"I'm fine, but I'm a mess," Nancy laughed. "Let me brush my teeth and comb my hair. Then I'll walk back to the store with you." She hurried into the bathroom.

Violet and Jessie waited in the big front room. "This room is just like ours," Jessie said. "I guess all the cabins are alike."

"But there's something strange about it," Violet said quietly, looking around. "I don't know what it is. But this room doesn't look right."

On the stone mantel of the fireplace were
two photographs in silver frames. Violet
walked over and looked at them. One was a
picture of a man and a woman. The second
was a picture of a young boy and girl. They
were standing near a tree, and the boy's face
was in shadow. But the girl's face was in
sunlight. "This girl looks a little like Nancy,"
Violet said. "But she has long, brown hair.
Nancy's is red and short."

Jessie didn't answer. She was staring at a
small shopping bag on the kitchen counter.
"Look," she said to Violet, pointing.

The bag was white, with green letters that
spelled the words *Elmford Shopping Center*.

Just then, Nancy came into the room,
ready to go. Jessie and Violet didn't say anymore to each other. But they both wondered
why Nancy would buy things at the new
shopping center when she knew how worried
Mr. Taylor was about it.

There were a lot of customers at the general store in the morning. But the afternoon
wasn't very busy. Violet decided to make a

new sign. When she finished, she showed it to Mr. Taylor.

"Something Aunt Jane said made me think of it," Violet told him. On the sign, she had drawn a picture of the general store. It looked just like the real one. Below the picture were the words, *Taylor's General Store. Old-fashioned Quality. Old-fashioned Prices.*

Jessie said to Mr. Taylor, "Aunt Jane said your things were just as good as the ones in the new shopping center. But not as expensive."

"It's a perfect sign, Violet," Mr. Taylor said. "Thank you. I'm going to put it out on that tree by the road."

"I'll help you hang it up," Henry said.

Violet went out with Mr. Taylor and Henry. Jessie stayed inside to help Benny fill one of the candy jars with sour balls.

"I haven't tried one of these yet," Benny said, as he held the jar steady. When Jessie was finished pouring the candy, he took a penny out of his pocket and put it on the counter. Then he popped a sour ball into his mouth.

"Benny!" Jessie said, laughing. "You should see the face you're making."

"It *is* sour," Benny mumbled because his mouth was full. "But I like it."

"I don't think there is any candy you *don't* like." Jessie was still laughing. But when she looked across the room, she saw Nancy, and she stopped laughing.

Nancy was standing by the shelves of clothes. A new shipment of T-shirts had arrived that morning. As Jessie watched, Nancy took a yellow shirt off the shelf. Then she rolled it up and tucked it under the shirt she was wearing. It hardly showed.

Jessie could hardly believe that Nancy was really stealing something. But she had seen it. She was so shocked that she gasped, and Benny heard her.

"What's wrong, Jessie?" he asked.

Jessie shook her head. She didn't want to tell Benny about it now. "I'll explain later," she said.

Just then, Mr. Taylor, Henry, and Violet came back inside. "Time to close up for the day," Mr. Taylor said. "Remember, Nancy, you have tomorrow morning off."

"I haven't forgotten, Mr. Taylor," Nancy said. "Maybe I'll go see a movie tonight."

Everyone helped to clean up the store for the day. As Henry swept the floor, he noticed that Jessie was very quiet.

"What's the matter, Jessie?" he asked.

"I asked her the same thing," Benny said. "But she wouldn't tell me."

"I can't right now," Jessie said. She looked at Nancy, who was nearby, dusting the counter. "I'll have to tell you . . ."

"Later," Benny finished. He made a face. "I'm always having to wait."

Henry smiled. "This time, we both have to wait, Benny."

Jessie tried to smile, too, but it was hard. She couldn't forget that she had seen Nancy Baldwin stealing from Mr. Taylor's store.

CHAPTER 8

The Visitor

That night, Benny got his pancake dinner. Jessie cooked bacon, too, which everyone liked. But when they sat down at the table, Violet noticed that Jessie wasn't eating much.

"What's wrong, Jessie?" she asked. "Do you feel bad?"

"Yes, but not the way you mean," Jessie said. "I saw something awful happen at the store earlier."

"Is that why you were so quiet?" Henry asked.

Jessie nodded.

"Well, tell us," Benny said. "It's 'later,' isn't it?"

"Yes, it is," Jessie agreed. "It happened while Henry and Violet were outside with Mr. Taylor. Benny was eating a sour ball and I was laughing. Then I saw Nancy. She didn't see me."

"What did she do?" Henry asked.

"She took a T-shirt from the shelf and tucked it under the shirt she was wearing," Jessie told them. "I watched her the rest of the time we were there, but she didn't take it out. When we all left, she still had the shirt hidden on her."

The others didn't say anything for a moment. They were as shocked as Jessie had been.

Finally Benny said, "How could Nancy steal from Mr. Taylor? He's so nice."

Violet looked troubled. But she said, "I just can't think Nancy would do something like that unless she had a good reason."

"That's what I keep thinking," Jessie said. "But what reason could she have?"

"Maybe she took the shirt because she doesn't have enough money to buy one," Violet suggested.

"But Mr. Taylor pays her," Jessie said. "And she has that ring, remember? She can't be very poor."

"Should we tell Mr. Taylor or Aunt Jane?" Violet asked.

"We'll have to tell someone soon," Henry said. "We won't be here much longer. And we can't leave without saying something."

"I know," Jessie agreed, pouring syrup on her pancakes. "But I wish we could solve this mystery ourselves."

Jessie ate some of her dinner. Then she stopped. "I just remembered something, Violet," she said. "The shopping bag. When Violet and I were in Nancy's cabin this morning, we saw a bag from the Elmford Shopping Center."

"If she can buy things there, then she doesn't have to steal," Henry said.

"She didn't buy much," Violet said thoughtfully.

"What do you mean?" Henry asked.

"Now I know what bothered me about her cabin," Violet said. "It was so empty, remember, Jessie? There weren't any books, or little knick-knacks, only those two photographs."

Jessie nodded. "Nancy said she has been on her own for a year. But she just doesn't have any *things*."

Henry shook his head in confusion. Then he snapped his fingers. "I just remembered something, too," he said. "The first day we were here, Mr. Taylor had to order more socks. He was surprised that there were so few left."

"And when he asked Nancy about them, she got real nervous," Jessie said.

"Then the next day, Jessie and I saw Nancy put money into the cash register," Henry continued. "And today she took a shirt."

Benny stopped eating. "I don't get it," he said.

Henry and Jessie had to laugh. "I don't either, Benny," Henry said. "This is a real puzzle."

"I like most puzzles," Benny said. "But not this one." He got up and took his plate to the sink. On his way back to the table, he glanced out of the front window. He stopped suddenly.

"What is it, Benny?" Violet asked.

Benny gestured for the others to join him. They did. Outside, they saw Nancy and Mrs. Edwards. They were walking together toward Mrs. Edwards's car.

In the morning, the Aldens were still puzzled. "I guess Mrs. Edwards and Nancy *do* know each other," Violet said, as they all walked to the store. "But I still wonder why Mrs. Edwards asked us about her."

"So do I," Jessie said. "And I didn't say anything about this yesterday, but when I saw that shopping bag in Nancy's cabin, I started to wonder if Mrs. Edwards and Nancy *both* might have something to do with the Elmford Shopping Center."

"What do you mean?" Henry asked.

"I don't know exactly," Jessie admitted. "Maybe they both work for the center in some way. Maybe they're spying on Mr. Taylor's store to see if he's losing business or something."

"If they are, that could be why Mrs. Edwards went to Nancy's cabin during our picnic," Henry said. "And why we saw them leaving together last night."

Violet looked upset. "I don't believe Nancy would do anything to hurt Mr. Taylor," she said.

"I have trouble thinking that, too, Violet," Jessie said. "In fact, I really *don't* believe it. But something funny's going on."

"It sure is," Henry said. "I hope we have a lot of work today. It will take our minds off of Nancy."

There *was* a lot of work to do. No one had a chance to talk about Nancy.

At ten-thirty, a young man came into the store. Jessie was measuring some material for a customer. Henry and Benny were in the storeroom with Mr. Taylor. Violet was putting bunches of carrots on the vegetable table.

"Good morning," said the young man.

Violet smiled shyly. "Good morning," she said. She was a little nervous about waiting on someone by herself. "May I help you?"

"No, thank you. I just came in to look around," the man said. He walked over to the building tools.

Violet finished with the carrots and went to the counter. The young man was still walking around. He had light brown hair and a friendly face. He looked familiar to Violet, but she couldn't remember where she had seen him.

After a few minutes, the man came to the counter. "Is Nancy here?" he asked. "Nancy Baldwin?"

"This is her morning off," Violet told him. "She'll be back after lunch."

"Then she *does* work here!" the man said. He seemed happy. "I'll come back later," he said to Violet.

"What's your name?" Violet asked. "I'll tell Nancy you were here."

The man sudddenly looked concerned. "No, please don't do that!"

"But . . ." Violet started to say.

It's a . . . a surprise visit," the man said, smiling again. "It would spoil it if you told her."

Before Violet could say anything, the young man walked to the door. "Remember," he called as he left, "don't spoil the surprise!"

Violet waited until Jessie's customer was gone. Then she told Jessie about the young man.

"I heard you talking," Jessie said. She looked worried. "He sounded afraid that Nancy might not want to see him."

"That's what I thought," Violet said. "But I wonder why she wouldn't. He was nice."

"I think we should tell Nancy about him," Jessie said. "She can decide if she wants to see him or not."

When Henry came out of the storeroom, they told him about the man. He agreed that they should tell Nancy about her "surprise" visitor.

A few minutes later, Violet stepped outside to shake out the dust cloth she'd been using. As she shook it over the side of the porch, she glanced down the path toward the cabins. There were two people standing in front of Nancy's cabin. One of them was Mrs. Edwards. The other was the young man who had been in the store earlier.

As Violet watched, Mrs. Edwards gestured toward Nancy's cabin. Then the young man walked up on the porch and turned the door handle. Violet gasped. The door opened, and the young man walked right inside!

Violet wanted to tell Henry and Jessie, but she didn't want to leave until she saw what happened. Before she could decide what to do, the young man came back out and shut the door behind him. From the way he shook Mrs. Edwards's hand, Violet could tell he was excited. In just a couple of seconds, the two of them walked to the end of the path and went into Mrs. Edwards's cabin.

Violet ran back into the store. "Jessie, Henry!" she cried, when she saw her sister and brother. "I just saw the man who was here, asking about Nancy. He was with Mrs. Edwards. Nancy must have left her cabin door unlocked, because he opened it and went inside. I thought for sure he was a robber, but when he came back out, he wasn't carrying anything."

As Violet told them what else had happened, Jessie and Henry looked worried. "Even if that man didn't steal anything, he shouldn't have gone into Nancy's cabin," Jessie said. "And I wonder how he happens to know Mrs. Edwards."

"I wish Nancy would hurry and come back," Violet said. "We have to tell her everything."

Later, Violet saw Nancy walking up the path to the store. "Here she is," she said to Jessie and Henry. "I'll tell her now."

Violet walked to the door with Henry and Jessie. But just as Nancy got to the front steps, a car pulled up and stopped quickly.

"It's him," Violet said. "He's back."

Nancy heard the car and turned around. The young man was getting out. "Nancy!" he cried. "It *is* you!"

The young man ran to the steps. "I have

to talk to you," he said to Nancy.

"Not now!" Nancy said. She sounded up-set. "Not here!"

"I won't go until we talk," the man said.

The Aldens heard Nancy sigh. "All right," she said. "I'll meet you later, after the store closes."

"Where?" he asked.

Nancy described the place where she and the Aldens had their picnic dinner. "But nothing is going to change," she told him.

"We'll see about that," the man said angrily. He turned around and walked toward his car.

The Aldens moved away from the door.

Just as Nancy walked into the store, Mr. Taylor came out from his office and asked her to go on an errand for him in Elmford. He gave her the keys to his van. Nancy waved to the Aldens and left the store again.

Violet looked worried. "What are we going to do now?" she asked.

"I know one thing we should do," Jessie said. "Nancy might need our help. When she goes to meet that man later, we should follow her."

"You're right," Henry said.

"Yes," Violet agreed. "No matter what kind of trouble Nancy's in, she's still our friend."

CHAPTER 9

A Secret Meeting

When work was over, Nancy quickly left the store. The Aldens said good night to Mr. Taylor and hurried outside. The young man's car was back. From the porch, they saw Nancy walking in the direction of the picnic spot.

"We should wait a couple of minutes," Henry said. "We don't want her to see us."

"Why not?" Benny asked.

Jessie put her hand on his shoulder. "We haven't had time to tell you, Benny," she said. "But you'll see."

"I hope I see soon," Benny said. "I'm hungry."

Violet smiled and held up a paper bag. "Mr. Taylor gave us some apples, Benny. You can have one now."

Benny took an apple and bit into it. Jessie, Henry, and Violet were too nervous to eat.

"Nancy is far enough away now," Henry said. "Let's go."

Quickly, but not *too* quickly, the Aldens walked toward the picnic spot. When they were almost there, they heard voices.

Henry pointed to a big willow tree up ahead. "We can sit under there," he whispered. "It will hide us, and we'll be able to hear."

They went to the tree and sat down under the hanging branches. Then they listened.

The young man was speaking. "You look different," he said.

"Not different enough, I guess." Nancy laughed.

Jessie felt a little better. At least Nancy wasn't afraid of the young man.

But the young man didn't laugh. He said,

"Why did you do it, Nancy? You're hurting everybody."

"That isn't fair, Tony," Nancy said.

"You're acting like a baby," Tony said.

Benny kept quiet, but his eyes got wide.

"I am *not!*" Nancy said.

"You're only nineteen," Tony said. "Do you want to keep hiding for the rest of your life?"

"No, I don't want to hide," Nancy said. Her voice sounded sad. "I just want everyone to leave me alone."

"Well, we won't," Tony told her. "We'll always find you."

Now Nancy sounded angry. "Not if I can help it!" she shouted.

The Aldens heard footsteps. Nancy was walking away. She passed by their tree, but she didn't see them.

"I don't care what you say, Nancy!" Tony called after her. "What you're doing is wrong!"

There were more footsteps. Then Tony walked by the Aldens' tree. From where she was sitting, Violet could see his face. It was shadowed by the leaves of their tree. Suddenly, Violet gasped. Now she knew where she had seen him before.

A few minutes later the Aldens were back in their cabin. They had seen the young man drive off. Now they were fixing a dinner of hamburgers and baked beans and fruit.

"What happened when Tony walked by our tree, Violet?" Henry asked as he poured milk for everyone. "I heard you gasp. You looked like you'd seen a ghost."

"Not a ghost," Violet said, putting the beans into a serving bowl. "It was Tony. And I'm pretty sure I've seen him before."

"Where?" Henry asked. "Today was the first time he came to the store, wasn't it? Where could you have seen him?"

"I saw him in Nancy's cabin," Violet said.

"Oh, I know!" Jessie cried. "The photograph on the mantel."

Violet nodded. "He was younger in the picture, but his face was in shadow, just like it was when he walked by our tree. I'm sure it's the same person."

"There was a girl in the picture, too, wasn't there?" Jessie asked.

Violet nodded. "She had light brown hair like the boy's. Like Tony's hair. But I'm almost positive it's Nancy."

"Nancy has red hair," Benny said. "*Real* red."

"She must have colored it," Jessie said. "Remember, Tony said she looked different."

"She probably cut her hair, too," Violet added. "The girl in the picture has long hair."

"You are so good at seeing things, Violet," Jessie said admiringly.

"But who is Tony?" Henry asked.

"Maybe he's her brother," Violet said. "In the picture, they looked a little bit alike."

"He might be her boyfriend," Jessie suggested. "Or just a friend."

"She didn't sound very friendly to him," Benny remarked.

"You're right, Benny," Henry said. "Nancy sounded mad. And she said she wanted everyone to leave her alone."

"Maybe she's running from someone," Jessie said.

"I just had an idea," Henry said. "Nancy told everyone she has been on her own for a year. But if she had been, she'd have plenty of things like socks and shirts, wouldn't she?"

"Yes," the others agreed.

"But if she was on the run, she wouldn't have enough things," Henry said.

Jessie put some ketchup on her hamburger. She started to take a bite, but then she set it down and sighed.

"What's the matter, Jessie?" Violet asked.

Jessie said, "Tony told Nancy that she's doing something wrong," she said. "Mrs. Edwards and Nancy both have bags from the Elmford Shopping Center. And they went somewhere together last night. I keep worrying that they're doing something to hurt Mr. Taylor's store. That would be wrong."

"But how would Tony know about that?" Violet asked.

"I don't know," Jessie said.

Henry thought for a minute. Then he said, "I think it's time to talk to someone about this."

"I do, too," Jessie said. "I'll feel a lot better when we know what's going on."

"I wish we could call Aunt Jane right now," Violet said. "But we don't have a telephone."

"Mr. Taylor has one in his cabin," Jessie said. "But he said he was going into Elmford for dinner."

"Then we'll just have to wait until tomorrow to call," Henry said. "But we'll take care of it the first thing in the morning."

Very early the next morning, Violet heard a noise outside their cabin. At first she thought it might be an animal. Then she heard voices. One of them was Nancy's. Violet sat up and looked at Jessie.

Jessie was awake, too. Jessie said to Violet, "Go wake Henry."

Jessie got out of bed and went to the window. It was just starting to get light. When she looked out, she saw Nancy and Mrs. Edwards. Nancy was dressed. Mrs. Edwards was in a blue bathrobe.

Violet came back into the room with Henry. "What's happening?" he whispered, tying the belt of his bathrobe.

"I'm not sure," Jessie whispered back.

The three of them stood close to the window and peered outside.

"Please!" Nancy said to Mrs. Edwards. "I have to get to town."

Mrs. Edwards shook her head. "It's too early." She sounded nervous. "Why don't you wait a while?"

"I can't!" Nancy said. "It's too important to wait!"

"I'm sorry," Mrs. Edwards said.

"Please," Nancy said again. "I *have* to go!"

Jessie looked at Henry. He nodded. If Nancy was going somewhere, they had to talk to her first.

The three Aldens opened the door and went outside. When Nancy and Mrs. Edwards saw them, they were surprised.

"Jessie, Henry, Violet," Nancy said. "What are you doing up? Did we wake you?"

"Yes, but we're glad you did," Jessie said. She took a deep breath. "Nancy, we need to talk to you. It's important."

"Jessie, you look so worried," Nancy said. "I don't understand."

"There are a lot of things *we* don't understand, Nancy," Henry said. "Things about you."

"About me?" Nancy bit her lip. "But . . ."

Before Nancy could say anything more, the door to Mr. Taylor's cabin opened and Mr. Taylor came out. He was dressed, but he looked very sleepy. "What's going on?" he asked.

"Oh, Mr. Taylor, I'm sorry," Nancy said. "I wanted to use a telephone, but I didn't want to wake you. So I was going to ask this lady to drive me to the nearest phone."

"The phone?" Mrs. Edwards said. "Why didn't you tell me?"

"I was in such a hurry," Nancy explained. "I couldn't think straight."

"Nancy, why did you call Mrs. Edwards 'this lady'?" Jessie asked. "We thought you knew her."

Nancy shook her head. "She gave me a ride to town the other night, but she never told me her name."

"I was afraid to say much," Mrs. Edwards said. "I was afraid you might guess who I am and why I'm here."

Nancy looked confused. "I don't understand."

"Neither do I," said Mr. Taylor.

"I think I understand a little of it," Jessie said.

"Me too," Henry said. "But not everything."

Nancy smiled. "Everybody's confused," she said. "I guess I owe all of you an explanation."

Just then, Benny came out of the cabin, rubbing his eyes. "What's everybody doing out here?" he asked. "What happened?"

"Good question, Benny." Henry laughed and put his arm around Benny's shoulder.

"And I think we're about to get some answers."

"Let's all go into our cabin," Jessie suggested. "We can have breakfast and talk."

Benny yawned again.

Henry laughed. "I said we'd take care of this first thing in the morning, didn't I?" he said. "And that's just what it is — the *first* thing in the morning!"

CHAPTER 10

Last Day at Work

Everyone started to go into the Aldens' cabin. But suddenly Nancy stopped. "I almost forgot," she said. "I need to make a telephone call. Mr. Taylor, may I use the phone in your cabin?"

"Of course you can," he said, gesturing toward his cabin door. "Go on inside, Nancy. The phone's on the wall, next to the refrigerator."

"Thanks." Nancy started toward his cabin, then turned back. "Don't worry," she said to the others. "I won't be too long. When

I come back, I'll tell you the whole story."

The others went into the Aldens' cabin. Jessie got out the things she needed to make pancakes. Henry took out glasses and started pouring orange juice for everyone. Benny and Violet put plates and silverware and napkins on the table.

Jessie was stirring the pancake batter when Nancy came back in. She was smiling.

"You look so happy, Nancy," Violet said.

"I am," Nancy said. "I just talked to my parents. I haven't spoken to them since I ran away from home."

"We were right," Jessie said. "She was running away."

Nancy smiled. "Why don't we all sit down and I'll tell you everything."

Everyone found a place to sit. Nancy sat on one of the chairs by the fireplace. She still looked very happy. "It was so good to hear my parents' voices," she said. "I can't stop smiling."

"You sound like you love them," Benny said.

"I do love them, Benny," Nancy told him.

"Then why did you run away?"

"Let me start from the beginning," Nancy said. "You see, my family is very wealthy," she explained. "There was almost nothing I wanted that I didn't get."

"That doesn't sound too terrible," Mr. Taylor said with a smile.

"No. I know I'm very lucky to have so much," Nancy said. "But there was one thing I wanted that I didn't get. That was the chance to make my own decisions about things."

"Like what?" Henry asked.

"Oh, about how late I could stay out and the places I could go," Nancy said. "My parents and I even argued about the kind of clothes I should wear. I felt like a baby. It seemed like they were always telling me what to do."

"And you wanted to decide things for yourself?" Jessie asked.

"That's right," Nancy said. "When I graduated from high school, they expected me to go straight to college. They even had the school all picked out."

"But you didn't want to go?" Violet asked.

"Actually, I did," Nancy said with a smile. "But it was just one more thing they were telling me to do. And I got stubborn and said I wouldn't go at all. We had some awful arguments about it. Finally, two weeks ago, I ran away."

"Two weeks?" Henry said as he passed out glasses of orange juice to everyone. "Then we were right. You never worked, did you? This is your very first job."

"You're right, it is," Nancy admitted. "But you sound like you already guessed. How did you do that?"

"Because you couldn't work the cash register or anything," Henry said. "If you had worked a lot, you would have known how."

"You're right," Nancy said again. She took a sip of juice. "I'm sorry I lied to you, Mr. Taylor," she said. "I needed the job so much."

Mr. Taylor chuckled. "I had a feeling you hadn't worked much," he told her. "But it's all right, Nancy. My customers liked you a lot."

"We all like you a lot, too, Nancy," Jessie said. "But we kept noticing things about you that didn't make sense."

"Like what?" Nancy asked.

Before anyone could answer, there was a knock at the cabin door. It was the young man named Tony. "I'm sorry to bother you," he said to Henry, who opened the door. "I'm looking for Nancy Baldwin. Have you seen her?"

"Tony!" Nancy cried. She jumped up from the chair as Henry let Tony in. "I called Mother and Dad," she told him. "I'm coming home. And then I'm going to college."

Tony looked very happy. "That's great, Nancy!"

Nancy turned to the others. "This is my brother," she said. "Tony Baldwin."

"We thought he might be your brother," Jessie said. "Or your boyfriend."

"You mean you've met?" Nancy asked.

"Not exactly," Violet said. "But I saw his picture in your room that morning Jessie and I came to get you. And when he came into the store yesterday, I recognized him."

"You sure did guess a lot about me," Nancy said. Suddenly, she looked at Mrs. Edwards, who had been sitting quietly on the couch, listening to the conversation. "I'm sorry," she said to Mrs. Edwards. "I know your name. But I still don't know who *you* are."

"I do, Nancy," Tony said. "Mrs. Edwards is a private investigator."

"Wow!" Benny said. "A real one?"

Mrs. Edwards smiled. She had a nice smile. "Yes, a real one," she said.

"Mother and Dad hired her to find you and keep an eye on you," Tony explained to Nancy. "They wanted to know you were safe."

"So that's why you went into her cabin," Violet said. "To make sure she was the right Nancy."

"And that's why I didn't want to drive you anywhere this morning," Mrs. Edwards said to Nancy. "You were in such a hurry, I thought you were running away again."

"Now I feel silly," Jessie said to Mrs. Edwards. "I thought you and Nancy might be doing something together to hurt Mr. Taylor's store." She told them about the shopping bags. "I'm glad I was wrong."

"I bought things at the shopping center because I didn't want to keep coming into the general store," Mrs. Edwards said. "I didn't want Nancy to suspect me."

"I bought my alarm clock there," Nancy said. "And a few other things. But I would never do anything to hurt Mr. Taylor's store."

"We know that now," Jessie said with a smile.

"I'm going to miss working there," Nancy said. "Even though I wasn't very good at it."

"What did Mom and Dad say when you talked to them?" Tony asked.

"They said they'd try not to tell me what to do so much," Nancy answered. "I didn't think they would be so understanding."

"It's like when we ran away from Grandfather," Benny said. "We didn't know how kind he was."

"That's right, Benny," Violet said.

Suddenly, Jessie jumped up from her chair

by the table. "Everyone must be starving," she said. "Let's have some breakfast."

"Tell me what else you figured out about me," Nancy said to the Aldens, as they started to fix breakfast.

While Jessie cooked the pancakes, she and the others took turns telling Nancy everything. They talked about how much trouble she had in the store and how nervous she got when they asked her about her family. Jessie and Violet talked about her ring.

Nancy looked down at her hand. She wasn't wearing the ring. "My parents gave it to me. I wore it because even though I was mad at them, I missed them, and it reminded me of them. But after you saw it, I put it away. It's a real emerald."

"That's what Jessie and I thought," Violet said.

"That made us think you weren't poor, like you said," Jessie told Nancy. "And Violet noticed that your cabin was bare," she continued, turning the pancakes over. "If you'd been on your own for a year, you would have had a lot more things."

"Things like socks and shirts, especially," Henry said. "Jessie saw you take the T-shirt. You didn't really steal from Mr. Taylor, did you?"

"Oh, no!" Nancy cried. "I wouldn't do anything like that. I took some socks and a shirt because when I ran away, I didn't bring enough clothes. I just didn't want anyone to start asking why I needed such basic things, so I took them. Then, later, I put the money in the cash register."

"So that's what you were doing," Jessie said. "Henry and I saw you but we couldn't understand why."

"And I couldn't understand why Tony looked so familiar when he came into the store," Violet said. "Then when we saw you at the picnic spot later, I remembered the picture in your cabin."

"You followed us to the picnic spot?" Nancy asked.

"We were worried about you," Jessie said. "We thought you were in some kind of trouble."

"We were afraid to ask you because we

thought you might get scared and run away,"
Henry said. "We wanted to help, but we
weren't sure what to do."

"You helped just by being my friends,"
Nancy said. "And you sure did figure out a
lot about me."

"We like mysteries," Benny told her.

"And *you* were a mystery, Nancy," Jessie
said.

Everyone laughed. Then Jessie said, "The
pancakes are ready. Let's eat!"

"Good," Benny said. He looked at Mrs.
Edwards. "Do private investigators like
pancakes?"

"This one does, Benny," Mrs. Edwards
answered.

Everyone got a plate, and Jessie served the
pancakes. They were all starting to eat when
Aunt Jane arrived.

"Aunt Jane!" Benny shouted, opening the
door for her. "Wait until you hear! We solved
another mystery!"

"Come eat with us, Aunt Jane," Jessie said.
"We'll tell you all about it."

When she had heard the story, Aunt Jane

smiled. "You all have certainly been busy," she said. "Working in a store *and* helping to solve a mystery."

"*And* being my friends," Nancy said. "I'll miss you all."

Violet asked, "Will you be leaving soon?"

"As soon as I can," Nancy said. "But don't worry, Mr. Taylor. I told my parents I couldn't go until you found someone to take my place." She laughed. "Thanks to the Aldens, I can *really* work in a store now."

"That's good, Nancy," Aunt Jane said. "But you might be able to go very soon." She turned to Mr. Taylor. "I found someone who wants to work in your store, Jerry," she said. "Her name is Jenny Parks. She just moved to Elmford, and she has worked in a lot of stores. She'll come out to see you tomorrow."

Mr. Taylor looked very happy. "Thank you, Jane," he said. "That's wonderful news."

After breakfast, Mrs. Edwards said goodbye and left. Tony drove into Elmford where he had been staying so he could pack his things. The others walked with Mr. Taylor to open the store.

"What a morning this has been," Nancy said as they all went inside. "So much has happened!"

"I told you we're always having adventures," Benny said.

"Yes, you did, Benny," Nancy laughed.

In just a few minutes, a customer arrived. She walked over to Mr. Taylor. "I just wanted you to know that I've tried that new Elmford Shopping Center," she said to him.

Mr. Taylor looked worried. "Yes?"

The customer nodded. "And your store is much better," she said firmly. "Your fruit and vegetables are fresher. Your fabric is just as good. And your prices are much better."

Mr. Taylor looked relieved. "That's very good to hear," he said.

"I knew your customers wouldn't desert you, Jerry," Aunt Jane said.

"I'm beginning to think you're right," Mr. Taylor said.

Aunt Jane was just about to leave when a man came into the store. "Hello, Dick," she said. "Look, Jerry, it's Dick Forest, who used to work here."

"Hi, Mr. Taylor," Dick said. He looked around and saw Nancy and the Aldens putting out fruit, dusting, and pricing things. "I see you have plenty of people working for you."

"As a matter of fact, I don't," Mr. Taylor said. He explained that Nancy and the Aldens would be leaving soon.

Dick looked very happy. "Then would you hire me again?" he asked.

"Of course I would," Mr. Taylor said. "But what about your job at the Elmford Shopping Center?"

Dick shook his head. "I quit, Mr. Taylor. I thought it would be a nice place to work. But the people who own it aren't very friendly. I'm just not happy there."

"Then you're welcome to come back here," Mr. Taylor said. "That way, we'll *both* be happy."

The Aldens smiled at each other. "Everything is turning out great," Jessie said.

"Now when we all go home, we won't

have to worry about Mr. Taylor not having anyone to work for him," Henry said.

"I'm glad," Violet said. "I can't wait to see Grandfather and tell him about it."

Benny went over to Jerry Taylor. "Aren't you glad, Mr. Taylor?" he said. "Now you have someone to take our place."

"I'm glad about Dick, Benny," Mr. Taylor said with a smile. He looked at all the Aldens. "But no one can ever replace the four of you."

"That's what Grandfather says," Benny told him.

"He's right," Mr. Taylor said.

Violet smiled at Mr. Taylor. "I'm glad everything is working out for you," she said. "Maybe I could make more signs for your store someday."

"That would be just fine, Violet," Mr. Taylor said.

"And maybe when we come to visit Aunt Jane again, we could work here, just for a day," Benny said.

Mr. Taylor laughed. "You're all welcome here anytime, and you don't have to do any work," he said. "But if I ever *do* need help again, I'll know exactly who to turn to."

"You can count on us *anytime*, Mr. Taylor," Benny said.

"Right," Jessie said.

"Yes," Violet said. "But now it's time to go home to Grandfather."

GERTRUDE CHANDLER WARNER discovered when she was teaching that many readers who like an exciting story could find no books that were both easy and fun to read. She decided to try to meet this need, and her first book, *The Boxcar Children*, quickly proved she had succeeded.

Miss Warner drew on her own experiences to write each mystery. As a child she spent hours watching trains go by on the tracks opposite her family home. She often dreamed about what it would be like to set up housekeeping in a caboose or freight car — the situation the Alden children find themselves in.

When Miss Warner received requests for more adventures involving Henry, Jessie, Violet, and Benny Alden, she began additional stories. In each, she chose a special setting and introduced unusual or eccentric characters who liked the unpredictable.

While the mystery element is central to each of Miss Warner's books, she never thought of them as strictly juvenile mysteries. She liked to stress the Aldens' independence and resourcefulness and their solid New England devotion to using up and making do. The Aldens go about most of their adventures with as little adult supervision as possible — something else that delights young readers.

Miss Warner lived in Putnam, Connecticut, until her death in 1979. During her lifetime, she received hundreds of letters from girls and boys telling her how much they liked her books.